UNSTOPPABLE BOY

BY

OCHEI INNOCENT

Contents

CHAPTER ONE

Life started on a golden note for Michael but went sour when he least expected. Wise men say you should never judge a race until the final whistle. Never count your money till the deal is done and dusted.

Michael was born with a silver spoon. At his birth, Michael's father was managing a gold mining company. He was born in one of the best hospitals on November 28, 1962. As at 1966 his father was already the Manager of a Radio Television Station in another town in the North.

Money was therefore not a problem. Everything looked very promising. For residence, they had a whole building to themselves in the Government Reserved Area. That is an area strictly reserved for high profile government officials and rich traders. Everything you could find in a five-star hotel was available in their home. They lived a high-class life of luxury and comfort.

Children of the home never lacked. They had enough to eat and plenty toys to play with. They only needed to ask for whatever they wanted and it would be theirs. The parents gladly provided because they had it. They had no less than three adult servants made up of two males and a female. Even the servants were well fed and clothed.

Once in a while their parents took them out. They went either to watch movies or visit friends. Sometimes they went to the big hotels just to swim and shop in the malls. Sometimes, they ate out.

Life was so sweet that it looked as if

nothing could ever go wrong.

But it did.

First, there was a ***coup-de-etat*** in the country. Some soldiers changed the government of the day by force of arms. In the process, they hurt so many people. Some felt the coup was not necessary.

Second, another set of soldiers carried out a counter coup. This led to more killings and agitations. People who had lived as neighbors suddenly turned against one another. Folks were then forced to flee to their respective regions.

In the end, a civil war broke out. The hostilities disrupted many lives and livelihoods, including those of Michael's family.

At the end of the war, the Federal Government granted amnesty to the rebel forces. It then proclaimed a policy of reconstruction, rehabilitation and reconciliation. Encouraged by this, the warring parties pledged to work and live together again as one family.

It was easy for the nation to pick up the pieces. The people forgave one and another and helped each other.

However, it was not easy for the individual families. Many lost so much that they did not know where to start again from. Yet, as Michael's Grandpa used to say, where there is a will, there is always a way.

 The family of Michael was part of those who decided to start afresh. As God would have it, his father was offered a job by the then Bendel State Government. It was not the kind of job Michael wanted but he had a family to feed. So he gladly took it up. They say a bird in hand is worth more than a thousand in the bush. It was a welcome palliative.

Yet, it was far from rosy again for the

family.

CHAPTER TWO

Michael's father left for the city. He went with his wife and other children but Michael had to remain in the village.

This was for two reasons. One, his parents were not sure the peace would endure. They did not trust the politicians to keep their words. They feared that the nation could return to arms any moment but the politicians later proved them wrong. Two, with their present salary, his parents could not afford a big accommodation.

Therefore, they asked Michael to remain with Grandpa. It was an easy decision. Everyone in the family knew that Grandpa was fond of Michael.

Two of the servants were also left in the village. They were tasked to help Grandpa on the farms until next harvest and planting season. It was expected that from the new season Grandpa would cut his coat according to his size by planting a farm only he could manage.

At this age, Michael had a young impressionable mind. He soon became used to living in the village. He accepted the fact that he had to share a lot of facilities with many people, unlike the time when they lived in the city. Then, each person had separate bathrooms to themselves to mention just one facility.

Here in the village, even the source of water was shared with others.

His parents tried to cushion the effect of the change. When they arrived the village, they accepted the things they met on ground. They took on menial jobs to ensure their children did not lack. They made sacrifices as parents.

Now that they went back to the city, reality stared Michael in the face.

Being observant, Michael quickly discovered two things. First, scarcity often leads to sharing. This is so because sharing is done when the thing on the table is not enough to go round. When sufficient, everybody is called to come and take as much as he or she wants. Michael was able to observe that each time a bush pig or something bigger is killed by the hunters, the village elders ask everybody to come and take as much meat as they wanted. No one bothered to share. However, when a goat is killed at Christmas, it had to be shared so that it could go round. One goat shared to an entire village can never be enough!

On top of that, Michael learnt that sharing leads to rivalry. Those who share were often found to have taken more than those who did not. As a result those who did not get enough often challenge those who share. Thus, giving room for quarrels and finger pointing!

Not long after this discovery Michael went to visit an uncle. As he came close to the house he overheard his uncle saying to somebody:

"The parents of that boy Michael do not even know that they are cursed!"

'They are just stupid' said the other person.

"Only cursed persons can return so empty handed?" said Michael's uncle said. "Some people returned with properties!"

Michael did not know how to react. He wanted to knock on the door and gain entry but his sixth sense told him not to. So he stopped and listened some more.

"You know these people who went to school. They do not know anything and do not ask questions from us who are in the village. So they learn the hard way. Michael's father may not even be aware that his elder brother from same mother was also sacked at the peak of his labor".

"He might not think of his elder brother at all! City people are so selfish!" said the other man.

'Do they ever think?' he further asked. 'All they know is carry the white man's book up and down".

'I know for sure that my brother's maternal bloodline is under a curse" said Michael's uncle who is a half brother to Michael's father.

Michael was shocked to the bone marrow. He could not believe what he was hearing. Two things bothered him. Firstly, his parents have always assured him that education is the key to success in life. Now he was hearing something different. He also found it bothersome that it could be true that his bloodline was cursed! They say in this village that no one under curse ever prospers!

 The people inside suddenly lowered their voices. Michael could no more hear them.

Instead of going into the house, he returned to his home.

As he expected, he met his grandfather resting on an easy chair by the entrance.

"Grandpa I want to ask you something" Michael requested after greeting him.

The old man knew immediately that something was wrong. Michael looked worried. His voice also was not stable.

Grandpa sat up. Michael was his favorite child. He loved the boy so much that he did not want anything to upset him.

"Ask me whatever you like Mike! I will answer honestly! Those who ask questions in life, never go astray."

'Is it true Grandpa that my father's elder brother lost his job when he was at the peak of his career? Was he sacked?"

Shock waves went through Grandpa. Being a hundred years old he had seen so many things and heard so many others. These things wizened him up. He knew immediately that somebody had been talking negatively about his heritage.

"Nothing like that happened! He died of a sickness. There was a contagious disease outbreak which killed many. It is not true to say he was sacked."

Michael had another question for him:

'Is it also true that my father also lost his job at the peak of his expectations?'

The old man cleared his throat first before replying. He found this uncomfortable.

"Listen, Michael! Do not allow anyone to confuse you. Your father lost his job because of the civil war. His brother died. It is very clear that both cases are not the same. One died, the other survived. If they were cursed, they would both be dead. The person who told you that is looking at life with negative spectacles. Such people often blame their stars or others for every misfortune and hardly see anything positive about living. In life, son, you must see things from the positive side".

 All this while, Michael was standing. Grandpa waived him into a nearby seat.

The old man watched Michael carefully. He could see worry still dancing on the boy's cherubic face.

"Sit down my son. I want to tell you something. I know that some evil person has been telling you something directly or indirectly. I do not care who that person is and do not want to know.

"As a father I have answered you honestly. Now I just need one thing from you"

Michael raised his eyes a little.

"Promise me that all your life you will not forget what I am about to tell you!"

Michael hurried to his feet and raised his right hand the way he had seen people on the television do when taking oath in courts of law. He could see that Grandpa was very serious.

"I promise you Grandpa that as long as I live, I Michael, shall never forget what you are about to say now."

'Then sit down and hear me well.'

Michael resumed his place on the seat bedside his grandfather's easy chair.

"The day is getting late. Therefore I will hit the nail on the head."

Michael said nothing waiting patiently for his grandfather to speak.

"I want to talk to you about life. It is full of ups and down. There is no man on Earth who succeeded without first failing at one time or the other. Temptations and trials will surely come one's way to success! They are natural. You must remember Michael that the only thing that brings lasting victory is determination. You must be determined to succeed. Never give up no matter what. If you fail, get up and try again. Until a person dies, no one can say he has failed.

"What I mean by this is that you must make up your mind to succeed no matter how many times you stumble or how many stumbling blocks are mounted on your road. Never discourage and never stop and from today, never listen to negative people again. Do you promise?"

'I do Grandpa.'

"I repeat Michael and I want you to always remember that stumbling blocks are part of the road we must pass through in life. They are there to test how determined we are to succeed. They are not to stop you. They are there to test your will. If you show them that you are determined, they will leave you alone.

"Those who do not love you would want you to believe that one disaster or challenge is enough for you to give up. Do not listen to what people say when you fall. Just get up and look for something new to do or a new way to do something you have done before!

"Thought there be a million tests on the road, the truth is that if you are determined to succeed, you will always find a way to overcome and pass through those things and have the last laugh on those who thought you can never succeed."

Michael expected Grandpa to talk some more but he did not. Instead the old man closed his eyes as if in deep sleep.

Michael waited for another five minutes but Grandpa did not move.

Just as Michael wanted to go the old man opened his eyes and said:

"Michael I know you wanted me to say some more things. Is that not so?"

'Yes Grandpa. That was why I waited'

"When I did not, when I pretended to be asleep, you gave up. Why did you not wake me up? You could have tapped me gently and politely asked if I had more to say but you gave up!"

His voice sounded bitter with disappointment.

"Now Michael that brings me to my definition of the word: determination. It simply means: when you want something, you never settle for less. If you have to ask questions, ask questions. If you have to run to get it or walk, then walk! Whatever you have to do, do! Provided you do not harm others to do it. Keep doing it till you achieve your goals. Do you understand what I have said?"

Michael nodded positively.

"Now I am an old man and very soon I will be gone to rest with my ancestors. Promise me you will not forget our discussion today and that in everything you will be determined to achieve your goals."

Again, Michael sprang to his feet, lifted his right hand and vowed:

"I promise you Grandpa that I will not allow anything to stop me from achieving my goals. If I have to run, I will run and if I have to crawl, I will crawl. I will not be discouraged by challenges on the road to success. I will do whatever it takes to succeed provided I do not harm other people."

'That's my favorite child!"

A bright smile appeared on Grandpa's face.

"Go and write down the statement you just made and bring it to me. I want to see it in your beautiful handwriting."

Michael quickly went and wrote the statement in his notebook. He brought it to his grandfather who still sat there waiting for him.

When he showed it to the old man, he smiled broadly and said:

"I am happy you have this. Read it every Saturday. Will you?

"I will Grandpa"

The old man pulled him close to himself and began to rub his head. Then he said:

"You are the light of this family and I know you will not let me down. I want you to know that I can now die as a happy man!"

That very night Grandpa died in his sleep.

While others were weeping and mourning Michael sat in a corner meditating upon the words of his grandfather.

CHAPTER THREE

A month after the death of his grandfather, Michael forgot all about what the old man told him. He also forgot the notebook. He could not even say where it was. All he could possibly tell you was that he knew where he kept it on the day the old man was buried.

However something happened that made him remember. For the past three years now he had been schooling in the village. His hope was that as soon as he sat for and passed the first school leaving certificate examination, his parents would allow him to attend a college in the city. That was the dream of every school boy of his time and age. In fact hid parents had promised him that much.

So he studied hard. He was always heads over his books and never failed to do his home works. Burning the midnight candle was his second nature.

Not that he really needed the extra effort. He was born with a sharp brain. In the past three years he had topped the class.

No matter who set the exam, be they internal or external examiners, Michael came out in flying colors.

As the days went by, the First School Leaving Certificate Examination came and Michael sat for it with other course mates. The exam was well invigilated and so no one could cheat even if they planned to. Almost all the students complained that the exams were quite difficult. Even some invigilators complained that the exam subjects that year were quite tough.

In the end the results were released. Many students failed not because the teachers did not teach well. Rather, most of those who flunked their papers were found to have paid more attention to gossiping and watching midnight movies instead of studying like other serious students.

Michael shown like a thousand stars. Throughout the Local Government Area, he was the very best. In his own school, he ranked head and shoulders above all. The school authorities praised him to high heavens. They said he had made them proud. Some of his teachers bought him gifts in appreciation.

As to be expected, Michael was quite happy. He looked forward to being in secondary school next year. He also looked forward to moving to the city with his parents. He bubbled with enthusiasm.

However, if wishes were horses, beggars would ride. He was taken aback when his father came home. After praising Michael for a job well done, the father pleaded passionately that Michael should repeat the class that he had passed so well. That according to the father, was to enable Michael's elder brother enter secondary school before him. Finances had so far kept the elder brother from secondary school.

The father also pleaded that the arrangement would enable him put his finances in order. He hoped to get a better job. Right now, he could not afford the fees for both sons.

Michael was devastated. He could not believe his ears. He had lived with high hopes. His father had been a promise keeper. So how could this happen?

Michael also loved his elder brother. He did not mind his elder brother moving ahead in education. He even pitied his brother that the war had made him lose some years.

That, however, did not change the fact that Michael was disappointed. He had hoped to make it to a city college this year. Michael could not stop the tears as it welled in his eyes. He wondered what he could do to make his father change his mind but at this point sadness made his mind blank.

After some hours of meditation, Michael

realized that there was no point crying over spilt milk. There was nothing his parents could do because money was involved. Even a goat would like to wear a necklace but who will buy one for it, he once heard his mother ask.

His teachers were very much disappointed. They too had high expectations. Not just because Michael was their best pupil. No! Michael going on to college in the state capital would have given them something to boast about. Only brilliant children of the time made it to first class colleges. Academically weak students gained admission mainly to rural schools in the days of Michael. Having an alumnus of their school in the city would have been a beautiful feather on their cap.

Yet they too could not do anything about it. The war just ended and everybody had one challenge or the other concerning money. The few scholarships meant for indigent students were taken up by those who had the connection.

Michael accepted everything in good faith. His father had since gone back to his base leaving Michael to lick his wounds. He decided to leave everything in the hand of God. He is the one who chases away flies for the cow without tail.

That was the second of a dozen wise cracks Michael got from his mother who never lacked comforting words. He hoped she had come to see him at a time like this. He knew that would be the exact thing his mother would say to dry his tears.

Once more he dusted his books. He resumed classes with others. It was the beginning of a new academic session. Every other person bubbled with enthusiasm, especially those who had just been posted to new classes.

Some of Michael's age mates in the village had counseled him to rather stay at home. They had argued that since

Michael had already passed the examination, there was no point repeating the class. Some said his father was just being wicked. Some of them complained so much that Michael politely told them that they should not cry louder than the bereaved. The cross after all, was his alone to bear.

Yet, one of them crossed the red line. He said he was sure that Michael's father was saving money to marry another wife. When asked what made him so certain about that, he asked:

 "Why would a big man in the city with only two sons in secondary school not afford the fee?"

 It was as if he knew how much Michael's father earned in the city and what the school fees were for secondary school student! As, the same fellow continued to run his mouth like a public tap, Michael asked him to mind his business.

 Unknown to Michael, while those boys

whined their mouths, one of the teachers that admired him so much was on his way to see him. The man came at the nick of time. It was as Michael was thinking things over. It was the man's visit that tilted Michael's decision.

Michael had once shared his memorable talk with Grandpa with this amiable fellow. On sighting the visiting teacher, Michael remembered the note Grandpa made him write before he died.

Michael quickly searched for the note, read it again and picked up courage.

When his friends came the next day to try and discourage him once more, he was ready for them. Michael told them that since the teachers were willing to have him back in school and since it was also something his father desired; he would obey his parents and teachers.

So Michael went back to school. He did not allow the scorn and mockery of his friends to stop him.

One day Michael was on this way back from school when he met his uncle.

"Where are you coming from young man? Have you not passed out already?" Asked the uncle.

Michael knew the question was not in good faith. He felt the urge to ask his uncle why he did not congratulate him like other elders in the village but exercised self control. He knew that his uncle was asking the questions out of mockery but that should not be an excuse for him to be rude to an elder.

Michael also remembered that the man was not his problem. He had since come to the conclusion that his problem was either his father got a better paying job or he, Michael, gains admission into a secondary school hopefully on scholarship.

With that, he kept his cool.

Politely Michael told his uncle that he was happy to be back in school because it would give him a chance to surpass his last result and get a scholarship.

His uncle laughed dryly. It was as if Michael had said something stupid. The man's stomach turned. Suddenly, he felt a great urge to toilet.

"Let me give you some advice" he said to Michael. "I can do with more hands on my farm. Why waste a whole year repeating a class you have already passed?"

He did not know that Michael liked farming. He did not know also that Michael had made up his mind that no matter what career he finally settles for, he must first have a degree. Therefore anything that would take him away from school before achieving that goal was not in his best interest.

'Thank you Uncle for your kind advice. I will find time to help you on your farm in between my studies but you know I still have Grandpa's farm to contend with."

'Well, I will be waiting for you and your father to come to your senses!"

Again his uncle laughed wickedly and rushed away. Recently, the mere sight of Michael made him either want to throw up or visit the lavatory.

CHAPTER FOUR

Michael's uncle did not let the sleeping dog lie. He was the type by nature that always wants to see the end of any matter. Not being happy at the progress being made by Michael, he decided to see a specialist in cursing people. He reminded himself that he had resolved that he would rather die than see Michael and his siblings succeed in life.

He went to the man very early in the morning. He left his home before people could either rise or recognize one another on the road. Even the cocks had not crowed. Only palm wine tappers had woken up to go about their business. They say palm-wine tappers and witches run shifts on top of trees. As witches are retiring to their homes, tappers would be taking over from them.

When the uncle got to the front of the medicine man's house he cleared his throat. He did this because the man's hut did not have a door. Therefore the uncle could not knock.

He cleared his throat twice before the person inside asked:

"Who is that?"

'A man you know but whose name you have not recognized'

"In that case" said the person inside, "As a regular visitor, you ought to know where to sit. I will be out in a moment."

Michael's uncle knew where to sit. There was a bamboo seat set under a tree to his right hand. He moved over there and sat down.

He did not have long to wait. His host came out under the minute. In his line of trade, practitioners wake up quite early. This is because those who visit them normally had to do so either in the night or very early in the morning. They never want people to see them coming to or from a man who never blesses but curses people for a fee. When close to where they would turn into his compound, visitors would first turn, look back and sideways before either entering or calling out the medicine man

They exchanged greetings. After that they settle down to business.

"You remember my half brother? The one that I always complain about?" John's uncle asked.

'How can I forget such a person? Have you not been here to complain about him uncountable number of times?' The witch doctor replied.

"Good. I want you to do something very simple about him this time."

'If the things I do are simple nobody will pay me for it?' objected his host.

He knew from experience that if people assume his task was easy, they would want to pay peanuts for such services. Such a thing would not be in his interest since he had a family to feed.

"I just want you to lay a curse upon his son Michael. The one that excelled in the last exam when many people failed"

'I have heard of him. This village is small and news flies faster than jet planes.'

"I cannot be alive and see him training his own children when he has refused to help me train any of my own."

The medicine man said that he understood but quickly asked for his fee.

'Our elders say you do not see a newborn baby empty-handed".

Being born and bred in the village John's uncle understood the native doctor's proverb. Quickly he dipped his hand into his pocket and brought out the required fee. Since they had been doing business together for a long time they both knew what was needed.

The host grinned from ear-to-ear after counting the money. Satisfied that it was complete, he consulted his gods and said:

"A basket does not go to the market and return empty. You shall have what you want because you have put dry firewood into a burning fire. Go home and relax.

The boy will fail every exam from today. The gods have spoken."

That made John's uncle very happy.

"Once he fails, I shall return to load you with money."

'In that case, I will start looking for where to heap the money because my curses never fail!"

John's uncle was so happy that he sang as he returned to his home. He did not care whether anyone saw him or not.

CHAPTER FIVE

Meanwhile, Michael continued to burn the midnight candle. He gave the teachers his ears and never failed to do his homework. He did not allow anything to distract him.

He also continued to do his house chores. He did them as quickly as possible so as to have time for his studies. For his age he was extremely disciplined.

 He did not take the forthcoming examination for granted. Instead he felt a burden. He knew from their comments and side talks that most of the students expected him to do better than before. He once heard two of his classmates arguing over the matter. One said since Michael had done the exam before the next one will be a piece of cake for him. The other one swore that he had heard of many persons who got to the hall and found that the exam questions were radically different and tougher.

John knew that those boys came close so that he could overhear them. They wanted to draw him into the controversy. However he had long made up his mind never to engage in unnecessary banter with busy bodies like those two. After all, birds of a feather, they say, flock together. Light and darkness have nothing in common.

He had quickly picked up his books and left in search of a quieter place of study.

Though Michael passed last year, he would not be the first person who came back to repeat a class after passing but who failed at the second attempt. Such people normally flunk the exam because they assumed they could always write with residual knowledge. Michael also knew that most of his teachers looked forward to seeing an excellent result from him. He knew that his head teacher in particular, would never settle for less! He liked Michael so much!

Most of the boys and girls were not serious with their studies. Instead, a set sneaked out at night to attend parties without the knowledge of their parents or teachers. Another group ran from pillar to post searching for ways to cut corners. They were willing to pay any amount to sit the exam by proxy.

How they came by such ideas Michael could not say. He had been told by his immediate father to only listen to his teachers and not his peers because a blind man does not lead another.

"If one's course mates have the right answers, then why are they students?" his father once asked him.

Michael listened as one came and said:

"Oh come mates; let us hurry to Lagos. The question paper has leaked. Let us go and get it before time.'

He counseled against but was told to mind his business, after all no one invited him. None of them dared invite Michael to contribute because they knew he was not only brainy, his family values would not allow him to participate in such things.

He saw the conspirators contribute money and select messengers to go purchase such "expos" as they were tagged.

Again, he warned them. Instead of heeding, they threatened to deal with him.

Michael could not believe such a thing was happening. Once, he pinched himself to be sure he was not dreaming.

It was on the day of examination that many realized that they had been scammed! Then, it was too late for them to reverse their self-induced fall to massive failure.

CHAPTER SIX

Something happened before the final exams.

None of the teachers knew that Michael had soccer prowess. They all thought of him only as a bookworm. No one could be blamed for that because his head was always buried in his books. His academic records spoke volumes of him as a budding scholar.

The fact that he could be useful to the school's soccer team got revealed at the nick of time. The school's Soccer Coach was grappling with a problem. He was short of strikers. Michael's school and Saint Mary's Primary School had a cup match at hand. As God would have it, most of the former players in Michael's school, had passed out.

Therefore, the Coach needed quality players to beat the Oppossing School but all he could lay hands were untested neophytes and a bunch of mediocre old hands!

The cup match was sudden. A well known philanthropist in the town, decided to celebrate his birthday in a big way. As one of the highlights, he decided to stage an inter-school competition. He planned it to be between the primary schools in the Local Government Area. That meant that a total of twelve schools would lock horns to decide the champion. That winning team would go home with a hundred thousand naira which was a lot of money at the time.

Michael's Sports Master, who automatically functioned as the Soccer Coach, quickly put together his team. His first choice number 10 was one of those who left the school last session. He had graduated.

The Coach consulted. One of the students close to him vouched to have seen Michael tapping the round leather somewhere in the village. The boy said Michael would be an asset in the school's team. That to the coach was like replacing an elephant with an ant. Michael was small statured and unknown as far as soccer was concerned.

Since he could not get a better offer the Coach decided to give the idea a try. He felt that not much was at stake since the match was a private affair. The Coach would have been worried if the event had been organized by the government.

For the players, much was at stake. Being selected at all was a rare chance to prove your mettle. There was no doubt that those who excel would have a regular place in school's soccer team! No one wanted to appear once and be set aside for better hands.

Also, the Philanthropist made some more promises. He pledged to give financial rewards to all participants. He earlier promised to bestow a trophy on the winner as well as each of the two runners-up! To cap it up, he promised to take members of the two final teams out on a shopping spree since Christmas was around the corner!

The twelve teams began in earnest to meet in pairs and to knock each other out. Before you knew it, the contest came down to the last two finalists and the highest goal scorer was Michael! He scored in all matches.

 It was a breath taking series of games and everyone looked forward to the grand finale!

Soon enough it was D-Day. The final game was between Saint Mary's Primary School and Michael's school namely St Theresa's Primary School.

Students of both schools came out in their numbers. They came to cheer their players to victory. They also came full of hope that they would share in the glory should their school win.

There was also a sprinkle of members of the public. Same came to watch the game. Others had different motives. The group that came to hawk light refreshments, could be seen with their wares, strolling round the field in search of buyers. Some ex-students of both schools could be seen too, mingling with players of their *alma-matta*.

Everyone believed that his own school would lord it over the other. There was great enthusiasm both in the pitch and in the gallery. Some students sang their school's anthem aiming to bolster the courage of their players. Even before the match started, some fans declared their favorite team the winner. Those ones danced lame even before the game started!

At 4:45 p.m. the referee blew the whistle for the take off. Immediately the two teams began to trade tackles. Both teams seemed to have equal ball possession. For the first fifteen minutes, it was a ding dong affair. No one seemed to have the upper hand.

There was a great display of skills between the two teams. Their ball possession was masterful and their distribution of passes a joy to behold as each team piled pressure on the other.

The fans were not idle. They played the ball with their mouths, scoring goals even before the ball was kicked near any of the two goal-posts! Assuming victory in soccer games is left only to the spectators and fans of the two teams, a million goals would have been scored in every match! While those who exhibited great skills were praised to the high heavens, those who did not do well were booed to no end.

In the end, Michael's school carried the day. They scored four un-replied goals. At some point, players of Saint Mary's seemed to have lost concentration. Thus, the goals poured in.

The result was received with mixed feelings. Spectators on the side of the winners said it was a massacre. Others said it was a miss-match! They wondered how the organizers allowed the agile boys of St. Theresa's to lock horns with the 'pregnant women' from St. Mary's.

Others decreed that from that day going forward soccer should be banned from Saint Mary's school. Only basketball and netball should be allowed, they insisted! That, according to them was because even a blind man could see that there were no boys in Saint Mary's.

All the boys there were nothing but girls masquerading as boys. Some even said that wearing of shorts should be forbidden and only skirts allowed in Saint Mary's!

To the great delight of many, it was Michael that scored a hat-trick. He got a brace at halftime and the other goal at the dying minutes of the game.

As the spectators and fans of the school left the field, they carried Michael shoulder high singing his praises all the way.

They were in-between the venue and their own school when they met Michael's uncle coming from his concubine's house. He asked one person what the celebration was about and they told him.

His countenance immediately changed. It was as if someone had given him a dirty slap on the face. You could see anger and pain dancing on his face. His blood pressure increased rapidly.

He so hated Michael that he never wanted him to achieve glory in any sphere of life. News of this achievement stung him like a bee.

Instantly, what gave others joy, became bile in his mouth! As is common with most enemies of progress, whenever Michael's uncle hears anything good about the latter, his face habitually falls in great disappointment and pain. This was neither the first nor second.

He immediately hurried home. He rushed again like a person pressed so much by nature. Anger and sadness mastered him as he headed home. People he met on the road were greeting him but he had no time for them.   .

Soon as he got home, he locked himself in. Then he pinned and sulked through the night, like a scolded spoilt brat. He locked himself indoors for seven days because he did not want to have any occasion to congratulate his blood brother's son. He chose to stay away till the ovation died down.

On Michael's part, life continued. From that day till he left the school, Michael never failed to play a full ninety minutes game for St. Theresa's team! With time, he became very famous both as a talented soccer wizard and a rare genius with his books!

Little wonder that when the terminal examination came, Michael shone again like a thousand stars! He did so well that each of the top three secondary schools in his state offered him tuition-free scholarships. His fame spread far and wide!

 The scholarship elated Michael. He knew it would be a great relief to his parents who had lost so much to the civil war. The scholarship could have been all expenses paid. The secondary schools were willing. However, their hands were tied by paucity of funds. If wishes were horses beggars would ride. Most of the schools could not afford a full scholarship. That was due to the fact that they were still rebuilding their structures and facilities destroyed during the last civil war.

When news of the scholarship got to Michael's uncle, it became the last straw that broke the camel's back. He picked up the rope with which he used to tap his palm trees for wine. He tested it and confirmed that it was still strong and study.

Quietly, he left his house. Foaming and fusing, he headed into the farm road. As he went along, he searched for a suitable tree. He had made up his mind to hang himself. He had long vowed to himself that he would not be alive to see Michael progress. He felt it was time to end it all.

CHAPTER SEVEN

Although Michael was very happy and full of high hopes, he soon found that the devil never gives up. That life is really not a bed of roses! It appeared to him that at every level he climbed, there was a demon waiting to throw spanners into Michael's work! That things are not always what they seem!

When his parents heard of his achievements they were indeed very proud of Michael. None of their other children had ever won a scholarship even for a year of schooling, not to talk of five years tuition-free scholarship! They felt very tall.

They reacted in more ways. First they knelt down to thank God in prayers. Next, they called in the neighbors and celebrated the good news with them.

Not done yet, the father left immediately to the village. It was a three hour journey full of potholes but he endured it all, smiling from ear to ear sometimes, much to the surprise of other passengers in the fifty-four sitter bus.

He went there to bring his hero to the city. As far as the father was concerned,

Michael had paid his dues. He no longer had any business being in the village. Since he had won a seat in one of the best schools in the city, the earlier he started getting used to the city pulse and environment, the better for everybody.

Michael's mother was very modest with her celebrations. She chose to do it indoors. She danced and hummed so many songs as she did her house chores all through the week. She paused from time to time to lift up her hands and thank almighty God for the mercy he had shown them through Michael.

On the contrary, Michael's father on his return from the village with Michael went to town with his celebration. He loudly beat his chest before everyone that cared to listen claiming that Michael took after him. Did they not know that an apple does not fall far from its tree? That every offspring of a snake must be long, lean and ropelike? Can a lion beget a tortoise, he asked any person with a listening ear.

Michael got some clothes and cash rewards! They came mainly from neighbors and friends of the family. These persons of goodwill came to celebrate with them as soon as they heard the cheerful news.

His father promised to buy Michael a motorbike should he do equally well in secondary school.

His mother immediately adjusted her food time table. She began to cook Michael's favorite dish. She did this each day for the next seven days much to the delight and satisfaction of Michael.

CHAPTER EIGHT

Michael accepted the scholarship. He chose one of the best high schools in the state. He had hoped and dreamed of attending this particular school. It was an old institution funded by the colonial masters. It had acquired a great reputation for its excellence in sports and academics. Merely being a student of that institution speaks volume of the endowments of such student.

Little wonder that students of the institution walk with shoulders high all the time. Among the alumni of the institution were serving and past governors. They also parade captains of industry and other notable professionals in the country. The list is of its alumni is a: ***who-is-who*** in the society!

Teachers in the institution feel very Olympic and professorial. They know very well, to date, that not every Dick and Harry can land an academic job in such a school.

It was therefore with great joy that Michael prepared to go to the school. He went to tailors and had his uniforms made as specified by the school while painstakingly having his old clothes washed and ironed.

His father purchased him a new suitcase and all looked set for him to go.

As the day drew for him to leave, he began to notice a shortage or total absence of some items listed in the brochure given to him for a place in the boarding house. His father would go out and return with none of the things Michael considered non negotiable.

One of such was an iron bed. Every student was expected to bring one in. The school had space but not enough beds. This situation was created by the quest of a large number of parents to get a place in the school for their wards. This put a lot of demand on the limited beds in the school. A second factor is again, a fall out of the civil war. Hoodlums took advantage to loot the school compound. They went away with almost every movable item including most of the beds and beddings.

This forced the school to ask the students to come with their own beds, pillows and bed sheets. Students had to come with foam mattresses and not cotton wool or rag filled mattresses. Grass filled mattresses were also taboo.

Foam mattresses were not easy to come by. They were beyond the reach of the poor and that included Michael's parents. They could not even get a fairly used one. Then, it was hard to see second hand household items on sale as is the case today. Those who had old furniture to discard simply donated them to poor relatives or charity homes. Today, even used, highly unhygienic tooth brushes are on sale!

Though the parents of Michael belonged to the middle class, they had ten other children to cater for. In addition to seven of their own biological children, his parents had three other kids to look after. These were kids inherited from various uncles within his extended family. Since Michael's father had adopted three, he found it difficult to take on a fourth child. "A man should not bite more than he can chew," he had told his wife on that occasion.

However, the uncle whose child was rejected became very bitter. The rejection became his lame excuse for going to various medicine men to lure them into cursing Michael and his siblings.

A major factor that added pepper to the matter was that most rural dwellers at the time, believed that people in the city were enjoying. They see urban dwellers drive into the village in expensive cars but do not know that most of the vehicles were bought on hire purchase with loans from governments and companies. Rural dwellers do not know that even the homes where people in the city dwell are on high rents per annum. Rural dwellers trek to wherever they wanted to. On the part of city dwellers, they have to hire drivers, burn fuel and maintain vehicles.

So too now: most of rural dwellers could not understand why Michael's parents could not afford an iron bed and foam mattress for him to resume in the boarding house.

Michael's parents did all they could to no avail. They knocked on various doors, yet no favorable response. Some fair weather friends told Michael's father that they wished he had come yesterday. They said somebody else had come and borrowed from them that yesterday. Now they maintained there was nothing left to be given out. Others gave flimsy excuses that could not hold water.

In the end, both parents decided to stop washing their dirty linen in public. That's what they considered it to be since people would listen to them narrate their financial woes only to refuse them what they the Michaels knew the person could well afford.

They decided to cut their coat according to their size. They asked Michael to choose either to start school next year or be an off campus-student in one of the third rate high schools within the vicinity, this year. He should please forget the scholarship he had received on a platter of gold.

Things were so bad that they made Michael to know that they could not even afford his transport fare on a daily basis to the school of his choice should he decide to be an off campus student! Were he to even be off campus, they would have to go into serious debt to cover his bus fares. Things were that bad!

For the parents, it was a bitter pill to swallow. It was the last thing they wanted for their child. However, they had no other choice. They ran out of ideas and contacts as far as the matter was concerned. There is a saying in their hometown which holds that when a man reaches the end of where he knows, his journey ends. For his parents their desperate journey to collect money from any source had ended.

They were highly pained by the fact. They knew that Michael wanted so much to attend that particular high-brow School. Yet, the parents had to face reality.

Michael's father, as a student in his time, read Chinua Achebe's book titled: ***"Chike And The River".*** In that book, the hero counseled that any Easterner who desired coming to Lagos but could not afford the transport fare, should settle for Asaba, a town on the western side of River Niger when coming from the East. The author said the advice was because half a loaf of bread is better than none!

Michael's father also knew another saying in his hometown which says that when a man hangs his hand where it did not reach, his ribs will start hurting! Michael's parents did not want their financial ribs to start hurting them. So they gave him those two options to choose from.

The whole situation confounded Michael. He could not help asking whether his parents would not have been able to pay his school fees into secondary school at all, if he had not gotten the tuition scholarship. Despite the fact of his pain and confusion, he asked the question aloud.

However, there was no one to answer him. He was alone in the room.

At a point, he wept like a baby!

CHAPTER NINE

Michael's uncle did not know that the medicine man was following him. Michael's uncle had been monitoring Michael. So too had the medicine man been monitoring Michael and his uncle. He did not want his client to do anything to harm the boy at the same time he owed his client a duty.

He had seen the aggressive change in Michael's uncle especially when news came that Michael not only excelled in soccer but greatly in academics. The uncle had come to him in the middle of the night. When hardworking men had not only gone to sleep but were in deep slumber.

He observed that Michael' uncle was full of fury. One side of his face shook as he talked.

The medicine man had managed to calm Michael's uncle down but he could see that he was capable of doing either Michael or himself harm. He knew that the man's hatred for his cousin had become obsessive.

 From that day he paid somebody to keep an eye on Michael's uncle. It was that fellow that alerted him. He reported that Michael's uncle was seen heading towards the farm road with a rope and a cutlass. Both men quickly rallied and followed the uncle closely behind without his knowing that anyone was on his tail.

They watched as Michael's uncle decided on a particular tree. He put his rope around the tree. They also observed him as he made a knot of the rope now tied to the tree and put the rope around his own neck while holding the tree. It was obvious that the man was trying to kill himself.

At that point the medicine man's spy quickly sneaked behind Michael's uncle and cut him down!

He fell heavily to the ground and passed out. He even soiled himself for the branch he used was quite high up.

He woke up in the local hospital. That was two hours later. His only sister, a police officer, and a nurse were there. The spy and the medicine man had gone into thin air. They wanted their identities to remain hidden.

Michael's father had been generous to his only sister. He had collected one of the woman's sons and had been training him the secondary school. Michael's father had also been sending feeding support to the lady and her indigent husband. These were some of the things that made it difficult for the man to train his own children.

So after being briefed on the cause of the attempted suicide, by those who rushed to her home that morning, she waited eagerly for Michael's uncle to wake up and get a fair share of her razor-sharp tongue! He even while he was in comma, she did not spare the man, calling him ingrate and many other unprintable names!

However when Michael's uncle woke up he was weeping heavily! This shocked medical staff, police man and his sister, who immediately forgot her sharp tongue.

CHAPTER TEN

When Michael woke up some days later, he noticed that he had over slept. He also observed that his father was in a meeting with some people.

They were talking in low tones but the apartment was not originally a three bedroom flat. It was one long hall now partitioned. The front room was separated from the other rooms with thin plywood sheets. It was therefore very easy for Michael to over hear what they were saying.

Michael guessed that there were about four persons including his father. One person whom he could not recognize from the voice was suggesting that

Michael should go and learn carpentry. Another person suggested that he should go learn how to repair automobiles. .

Just as Michael was about to resume his weeping, he heard an angry voice hushing others down. Michael moved closer to the door and listened intently. A man was talking.

"The Michael I know is too intelligent for all the trades that you are suggesting. Why would he have to go that way?"

Michael realized that no one was countering the man. Presently the man continued:

'Have you people forgotten that the boy you are talking about is my godson? Am I not the one that stood as his Spiritual Father on the day of his water baptism?"

This was followed by a few minutes of silence. It appeared no one had forgotten as their silence seemed to indicate. One or two actually nodded in agreement but Michael was not in a position to see that. All he knew from his position in the other room was that the man continued unchallenged.

"If it is bed that will stop this brilliant young man from going further in his education or to a school of his choice, then I will give up my bed. Let him go to school with it. It is exactly the type prescribed for the students of the school and as you know my wife is still in the village. So there is no one to object."

"That solves the problem!" said one of the people present. He barely allowed the other man to finish talking.

"What else are we looking for? The head of the stubborn goat has fallen perfectly into the bag purchased to hold the head of stubborn goats!"

Michael could hear two other persons speaking out in full support of the donation. Michael's joy knew no bounds.

Just as joy was overflowing Michael's heart, he had the donor speaking again.

"There is actually one drawback" There was something about his voice that gave Michael goose pimples. The man himself looked greatly pained.

"And what can that possibly be?" Michael's father asked his heart beating faster.

"In fact, that has been the only reason why I did not make the offer earlier. I have been worried about it!'

"Stop beating about the bush, my friend. Tell us what is there to worry about?' One other person challenged eagerly.

"One of the legs of the bed is not okay. Each time I try to set it up on its four legs, it capsizes! So to keep it steady and standing, I usually put a small wooden stake in between the legs of the bed. That would have been embarrassing to me, were it in my parlor but thank God it is in my bedroom: seen only by me.

"I wonder if other students will not make a mockery of Michael in the boarding house with such a bed that has to be propped up with a piece of wood!"

For a moment those in the sitting-room were silent as they considered this new information.

Michael could not wait. He rushed out to the sitting room and prostrated on the floor in appreciation of the donor and his donation. Tears of joy ran down his young face.

"Thank you so much uncle", he said to the man. "I do not mind being mocked at all. What is important to me is that I am able to go to secondary school and take up the scholarship given to me. Even if the whole school laughs at me because of my bed, I promise that I will not mind them. Please just let me have the bed and go to school".

The donor smiled broadly for he was indeed happy to be of help to his godson. He heaved a sigh of relief.

'In that case follow me to my house immediately and take the bed. Giving you the bed is the least I can do for you but promise me that you will continue to pay attention to your studies.'

Michael could not stop the tears of joy as he vowed to be an excellent student in school.

Things happened fast. His father went with Michael. Together, they carried home the bed. The donor added some small change for Michael "to buy bread" on the way to school. Michael had already lost a week at home. So his parents quickly arranged for him to be in school next day.

Coincidentally it was the day Michael reported to school that his uncle woke up from coma. When asked what he was weeping for, he explained that while he was in coma, he saw himself in what looked like a dream appearing before his dead father.

The old man severely rebuked him for being both wicked and selfish. According to him the old man ordered some fierce looking and able-bodied men around, to lie Michael's uncle down and give him forty lashes of the cane! He said they could have continued flogging him if not that he cried out desperately and promised to turn a new leaf.

He further said that his dead father made him swear that if given a second chance, he would love every child on earth like his own son, not minding who their parents are. He also swore to be grateful for every good thing that happens to him and not blame others for not helping him.

 His sister did not spare him despite his tears. She scolded and reminded him of how the same brother he was going up and down trying to curse had been the one who paid for him to learn a trade and the one who singe handedly ensured that all his other brothers learnt one trade or the other.

The uncle swore that he had repented of his sins. He promised to be a better uncle to Michael in particular.

On his part, Michael went on with his life. He spent five event full years in secondary school. After which he graduated in flying colors. He then proceeded to the university on Federal Government scholarship! Though he faced many other obstacles, he overcame them all.

In the university, he broke many academic records. The university retained him as a Research Assistant doing a Masters Degree course while helping his professors in research work! He then proceeded to his youth service without ever missing a step again.

Many things and persons had tried to stop him but Michael proved to be unstoppable!

OTHER SHORT STORIES BY OCHEI INNOCENT

1. FROM SCHOOL TO PRISON
2. STUPID GIRLS
3. NOT A SIMPLE MATTER
4. AMBUSHED; BETWEEN THE DEVIL AND THE DEEP BLUE SEA.
5. HUNTED ON ALL SIDES
6. DIMKOLO

ABOUT THE AUTHOR

OCHEI INNOCENT ENJOYS TELLING STORIES MORE THAT EATING.

HE LIVES IN NIGERIA AND IS MARRIED WITH FOUR KIDS.

THANKS

You can contact me on:
newochei@gmail.com.

I will be very glad to read your reviews and suggestions on how to improve.

Thanks in anticipation.

Ochei Innocent.